W9-CIA-846

E
Par

Parish, Peggy
Thank you, Amelia
Bedelia

DATE DUE		
NO 21 '85	JY 19 '90	MAY 11 '94
JA 9 '86	JY 3 '91	JN 20 '95
MY 15 '86	JY 25 '91	NOV 1 3 '95
SE 13 '86		JUL 1 5 '96
FE 13 '87	AG 23 '91	MAR 5 '97
MR 1 8 '87	JA 3 '92	JAN 2 3 '99
JY 8 '87		APR 2 2 '99
DE 13 '88		MY 17 '00
MY 27 '89		JE 28 '02
AG 29 '89		JY 12 '02
JE 25 '90		JY 26 '06
		JE 30 '07 MY 25 '10
		JY 30 '14 AU 0 1 '22

MEDIALOG
Alexandria, Ky 41001

Thank you, Amelia Bedelia

by Peggy Parish

Pictures by Fritz Siebel

HARPER & ROW, PUBLISHERS
NEW YORK, EVANSTON, AND LONDON

A Harper Trophy Picture Book

For Ann, Jack, and Brad Rost

Mrs. Rogers was all in a dither.
"Great-Aunt Myra is coming today."
"Now, that is nice," said Amelia Bedelia.
"I do love company."
"We've been trying for years to get her to visit,"
said Mrs. Rogers. "But Great-Aunt Myra says the only
place she feels at home is at home.
So everything must be exactly right.
We do want her to be happy here."

"Now don't you worry your head," said Amelia Bedelia.
"I'll fix everything. What should I do first?"
"Well, the guest room must be made ready.
Strip the sheets off the bed. Remake it with the new
rosebud sheets," said Mrs. Rogers.
"Thank goodness you're here."

Amelia Bedelia went to the guest room.
"These folks do have odd ways.
Imagine stripping sheets after you use them."

Amelia Bedelia shook her head.
But she stripped those sheets.

Amelia Bedelia had just finished when the doorbell
rang. "That must be the laundryman with Mr. Rogers'
shirts," called Mrs. Rogers. "Please check them and
make sure they're all there."
Amelia Bedelia hurried to the door
and took the package.

Amelia Bedelia opened the package.
She unfolded each shirt.
"Two sleeves, one collar, one pocket, and six buttons.
Yes, they're all here. There's not a thing missing,"
said Amelia Bedelia.

"Now to check them.
It would be a sight easier to buy them already checked,"
said Amelia Bedelia.
But she quickly checked each shirt.

Mrs. Rogers came downstairs in a rush.
"Amelia Bedelia, my bright-pink dress has spots in it.
Please remove them with this spot remover.
Leave the dress out. I will wear it tonight.
Now I must go to the market."

Amelia Bedelia looked at the bright-pink dress.
"I don't see any spots. This dress just needs washing."
Then another dress caught Amelia Bedelia's eye.
"She must have meant her light-pink dress.
Now that one sure is spotted."
Amelia Bedelia held the dress up.
"It looks mighty nice with the spots in it.
But I guess she's tired of it that way."
Amelia Bedelia put spot remover on each spot.
Then she waited.

Nothing happened.
"Didn't think that stuff would work,"
said Amelia Bedelia.
She got the scissors.
And Amelia Bedelia removed every spot
from that dress.

"Amelia Bedelia," called Mrs. Rogers.
"Please take these groceries."
Amelia Bedelia ran to take the bag.
"Here are some roses too.
Do scatter them around the living room.
I must get my hair done now.
While I'm gone, wash all the vegetables and
string the beans.
If you have time, make a jelly roll.
Great-Aunt Myra does love jelly roll,"
said Mrs. Rogers.

Amelia Bedelia stopped in the living room.
"Seems like roses would look nicer sitting proper-like
in vases. But if she wants them scattered,
scattered they will be."

Amelia Bedelia went on to the kitchen with the groceries.
She washed all the vegetables.
Then she found a ball of string.
And Amelia Bedelia strung all those beans.

"Jelly! Roll!" exclaimed Amelia Bedelia.
"I never heard tell of jelly rolling."
But Amelia Bedelia got out a jar of jelly.
Amelia Bedelia tried again and again.
But she just could not get that jelly to roll.

Amelia Bedelia washed her hands.
She got out a mixing bowl.
Amelia Bedelia began to mix a little of this and a
pinch of that.
"Great-Aunt Myra or no Great-Aunt Myra—
There's not going to be any rolling jelly in this
house tonight," said Amelia Bedelia.

Mr. and Mrs. Rogers arrived home at the same time.
Mrs. Rogers called, "Amelia Bedelia,
please separate three eggs
and pare the other vegetables you washed.
I'll do the cooking."
Then she and Mr. Rogers hurried upstairs to dress.

Amelia Bedelia took out three eggs.
"I wonder why they need to be separated.
They've been together all day and nothing happened."

But Amelia Bedelia separated those eggs.

"Pair the vegetables!"
Amelia Bedelia laughed.
"Here, you two go together—and you two.
Now be careful or I'll be separating you, too."

Amelia Bedelia went up to Mrs. Rogers' room.
"What should I do with these stripped sheets?"
she asked.
"Stripped sheets!" exclaimed Mrs. Rogers.
But she got no further.

Mr. Rogers roared, "What in thunderation happened to my shirts?"
"Oh, don't you like big checks?
I didn't have time to do little ones.
But I will next time," promised Amelia Bedelia.

"My dress!" exclaimed Mrs. Rogers.
"It's full of holes."
"Yes, ma'am, I removed every single spot,"
said Amelia Bedelia.
Before Mrs. Rogers could say any more,
the doorbell rang.

"Great-Aunt Myra," said Mr. and Mrs. Rogers.
They rushed to the front door.

"Good evening, grandniece.
Good evening, grandnephew.
My, that trip made me hungry," said Great-Aunt Myra.
"I'll cook dinner right now," said Mrs. Rogers.
Everybody went into the kitchen.

"Amelia Bedelia, did you string the beans?"
asked Mrs. Rogers.
"Yes. See—they do give such a homey look,"
said Amelia Bedelia.
"Where are the eggs I asked you to separate?"
said Mrs. Rogers.
"Here's one, one is behind the clock, and the other
is over there.
Did I separate them far enough apart?"
asked Amelia Bedelia.

Mrs. Rogers said nothing.
So Amelia Bedelia went on.
"And I paired the vegetables.
They went together real well,
and there weren't any left over."

Mrs. Rogers slapped her hand on the table.
It hit right in a sticky blob.
"Ugh! What is that?" she shouted.
"Jelly. I tried to make it roll.
But it just plip-plopped all over the place,"
said Amelia Bedelia.

"Amelia Bedelia!" exclaimed Mrs. Rogers.
"How do you get things so mixed up?"
"Things mixed up! Oh, I plumb forgot,"
said Amelia Bedelia.
She hurried to the stove.

Amelia Bedelia opened the oven door.
Great-Aunt Myra sat up straight and sniffed.
"Hot apple pie! I do declare.
Now that's the kind of mixed-up thing I like."

Great-Aunt Myra announced, "Grandniece,
grandnephew, I like it here."
"Oh, Great-Aunt Myra, we're so glad!"
said Mr. and Mrs. Rogers.
They both began to talk at once.
But Great-Aunt Myra wasn't much for words.
She had her eyes on that last piece of pie.

Great-Aunt Myra put the last piece of pie on her plate.
Then she said, "Grandniece, grandnephew,
I will visit you often.
That Amelia Bedelia really knows how to make a body
feel at home. Thank you, Amelia Bedelia."
Amelia Bedelia smiled.
She and Great-Aunt Myra would get along.